Carers'
Kaleidoscope

A selection of
poetry and prose
from
Signpost Creative Writing
Group

'Remember, you are not a saint, you are simply human - but you were there, and you cared'

Introduction

This anthology has been written by carers and ex-carers who have attended creative writing workshops at The Heaton's Centre since 2018.

We have used different prompts to inspire our writing including rewriting a fairy story from a different point of view as you will see in, amongst others, *Glass Slippers* by Rob Tuson, and *Beauty is in the Eye of the Beholder* by Jo Bennett.

Many of the stories and poems are based on personal memories as in *A Feast of Memories* by Maggie Waker who writes about being introduced to Vesta curries for the first time and *Memories of Home by Arthur Spedding.*

The group were asked to choose a coloured button that would either transport them to anywhere instantly, make them invisible or give them the power to read minds. In *Choose Your Button Annette* chose the grey and yellow buttons to get an instant tidy in her garden.

The lockdown of 2020 due to Covid 19 meant that we could not meet in person but did manage to keep going via Zoom. Unsurprisingly, some of the work the group have done was inspired by the lockdown situation as in *The Covid Cokey* by Caroline Bradley.

We hope you enjoy this anthology. We have written about our caring roles, memories from the past, stories with children in mind and number of limericks that we hope will make you laugh.

All the profits from the sale of this anthology will be given to Signpost to further their work with carers in Stockport.

Thankyou from Signpost Creative Writing Group 2021

What Being a Carer Means to Me
by Anne Thompson

Often there are days when I need more than my fair share of patience,
but sometimes there's
a good that really lifts my heart. Compassion and concern go with the
job title and occasionally
a sense of humour can really reduce the stress levels and diffuse a
tense and awkward situation.
Yes, being a carer isn't easy but with a good support network it is
much less daunting.

Caring Cinquain
by Anne

Caring
can be hard, but
something even harder
is finding time to take care of
myself

Recipe for a dream by Maggie Waker

The ingredients
2 litres of hope
4 grams of happiness
One block of help
A tub of energy
8 hours of sleep and
Five magic pills or more as needed

Method
Take 8 hours of sleep cooked well in a warm and cosy bed.
Carefully add the happiness incorporating throughout the day.
Divide the help into four equal pieces and add very gradually to the mixture.
Warm the hope and melt slowly in a pan.
Pour over the mixture allowing it to slowly spread around.
Take as many magic pills as needed, adding as necessary.
And stir in the energy.

Growing Old Disgracefully by Anne Thompson

When is one considered old? When I was twenty old was forty, at forty it was sixty. Now I am in my seventies it's not when does old begin, but more what is old.

I will never grow old gracefully. I shall always try to wear fashionable, not necessarily comfortable clothes, and shoes, never mutton dressed as lamb, more a sense of elegance. Grey hair is not an option, it does not go with my colour toning. Music energises me, so I cannot see myself not enjoying a good dance and doing Zumba with my other young "old lady" friends.

My teenage granddaughters tell me they cannot imagine me being a rosy cheeked Grannie and I hope they are right. If I ever need a walking stick, may it be psychedelic, my glasses will be trendy, my hearing aid unobtrusive. My sensible shoes will be customized with bows and sparkle, and my toes and fingernails painted with acrylic varnish. Any arthritic aids I may use will be hand painted and my stair lift will resemble a roller coaster.

I think I know what growing old is to me. It is not understanding technology, being unable to unravel problems on my smart phone or laptop, not being fluent with spreadsheets and having difficulty cutting and pasting. Will this worry me when I am sitting in my favourite restaurant enjoying a good meal (I am glad I have taken care of my teeth over the years) and drinking a glass of prosecco in my designer elastic waisted trousers. I think not.

As I write this, I am looking at a photograph of my grandma, younger than I am now when it was taken, and I know under her dress she wears boned and laced corsets and directoire knickers. How far we have come. Seventy now really is the old sixty or less.

The Misunderstanding by Annette Pickering

The emaciated figure huddled in the corner.

Joe had lain there for what seemed like many hours. He didn't know what time it was. They had stolen his watch. The fire he had struggled to light on his arrival was now burnt out and he was chilled to the bone.

Joe raised a gnarled hand to his face feeling the congealed blood now dried and hard on his wizened skin. He began to tremble as he thought about his perpetrators. They had ignored his pleas as he begged for mercy while they rained bludgeoning blows down on his head with their weapons.

He could still hear their cracked laughter echoing through his brain, as they ran off, leaving him for dead. Why did they do it? They couldn't have been more than fourteen. The same age as his grandson, Mark.

Mark was the reason he had gone out for a walk in the first place. It had been Friday night after dinner. He'd overheard the child talking to his parents, "Can I have a bedroom to myself instead of sharing with Granddad?" Joe had not stayed long enough to hear any more, he'd pulled his coat from the hook in the hall and left.

Mark was right. He shouldn't have to share a bedroom with an old man, not at his age. Fourteen was the age to have friends to stay. Sleepovers they called them now. Though from what he had heard there was very little sleep took place.

Joe had wandered aimlessly for a couple of hours oblivious to the rain dribbling down the back of his neck. His head down against the icy wind, he had not noticed the group of young lads spread right across the footpath, until he bumped into them. "Watch where you're going, you daft old bugger." One of them had said. "People like you should be in a home."

"You're too old to be out in the woods at this time of night."

Before Joe had time to respond, the youths had pushed him to the ground and were hitting him with sticks.

Only when they had run off, did Joe manage to crawl to the derelict cottage. He'd seen the cottage before on one of his many country walks during the summer months. It had reminded him of the many happy years he and Ellie had spent together before the cancer had cruelly snatched her from him, and illness that had made it impossible for him to cope on his own. Leaving him with no option but to accept the invitation from his daughter and son in law, to move in with them.

Joe drifted in and out of sleep, unaware of time. He knew it was night because it was still dark.

At dawn, he would drag himself into the forest to gather wood to make a fire. The ensuing heat would bring comfort and warmth to dry his wet clothing. He was hungry now, but the energy that he'd had as a young man was drained from his frail form. The wind whistled through the glassless windows of the rotten frames, as Joe drifted off again.

In his dream, Ellie was with him, not just the photograph that lived in his pocket, but there with him. Young and beautiful. Just as she had been on the day, he returned from the vicious battles of war so many years ago.

Joe's reverie was disturbed by the sound of church bells. It must be Sunday. How long had he been there? In the distance he could hear shouting. He moved his hand subconsciously to his pocket. "It's going to be ok Ellie," he murmured. "They want me back."

The shouting came closer. The rustling of leaves crunching as footsteps neared the cottage. "Dad, he's in here, Granddad's here. I've found him, I've found him. Can I tell him about the extension?"

Resolve by Linda Scholes

Things, stuff, keepsakes, memorabilia,
too much my family says,
a mountain,
time to declutter,
okay so today is the day
starting at the top
in the attic.

And there, piled high
boxes of memories
bound by strings of nostalgia
with ribbons of deep feelings
tying them to me,
cut those bonds, break free move on
where shall I begin?

In a dusty corner, a sack,
a torn and tattered plastic bag,
drag it forward
that mystery bag.
Its contents spill out
crushed, crumpled, creased
across the floor.

Of course, I remember now,
Mother's good wool coat
bought in the sale
from Manchester one winter,
how proud she was
of its quality, its timeless style,
its Kendal Milne label.

Faded grandeur,
the deep plum coloured material
no longer rich and vibrant,
inside a pocket, a hankie
embroidered with a letter "E",
a Foxes Glacier Mint
stuck to the lining,
a coin or two.

And when she died
I looked for comfort, wrapping myself
around in warm folds,
a sweet scent of lavender
reminding me of my mother but,
the years have past
and now.

This is just an old coat
of no use except,
there on the collar
some grey hairs lie,
gently and respectfully
I pack up the precious find
and replace it carefully in the bag.

I think that's more than enough
for one day,
mustn't overdo it,
I can always start again,
maybe tomorrow
or even the next day
perhaps next week………

Dreams by Annette Pickering

I dream of a time long gone when my memory held a bucket full of vocabulary and the words spilled from my brain to my pen.
Dribbling reams of platitudes onto the crisp white page.
But instead, now there is barely a cupful.
Each word has to be carefully thought about before it limps its way from my sometimes shaking hand.

Doppelganger by Arthur Spedding

Just as I arrived at the bus stop, I saw the last bus of the evening drive off leaving me stood in the pouring rain. I looked up at the departing bus and saw at the rear window a man staring back at me. "My God, he looks like me," I said to myself.

I'd been working late at my office catching up on some paperwork. Normally I would have driven home but my car was in for repair at my local garage, so I now faced a long walk home in the rain. Turning up my coat collar to keep out the rain, I set off for home.

It was an hour or so later that I was walking up the garden path towards my front door. I couldn't find my keys as I fumbled in my coat pocket, so I pressed the front doorbell. Through the front door glass, I could see my daughter, Sophie walking up the hallway towards the door. "Hurry up Sophie," I shouted. "It's chucking it down out here."

She opened the door, took one look at me, turned, and shouted down the hallway, "Dad," and looked back at me with a frightened expression on her face. Suddenly from behind her a face appeared. It was the face of the man I'd seen earlier on the last bus. He looked at me over her shoulder and with a strange smile on his face said, "Can I Help you?"

All Problems Eliminated by Jean H

"Why does she do this, doesn't she realise that her behaviour is driving you away?"

We were walking beside the Bayou on a warm balmy evening hand in hand watching the evening birds catching bugs on the wing.

"I know and it hurts me so much, but what can I do"? came the reply.

After saying that, I let the matter drop as I could see it was upsetting her. We walked on and made arrangements to meet up the following night.

I could picture the scene as she got home. "Where have you been, gallivanting with that man again. Don't you dare bring him here I will not have trash on my doorstep and don't look at me like that!"

In my office the following morning looking at an empty diary, the phone rang. I answered with my usual welcome. "All Problems Eliminated."

"Er, I have a problem with my daughter and as your business says, *Problems Solved.*"

I suggested that she came into the office that afternoon to discuss any proposals she might have, but I forgot to ask her name. At 2.30 pm, there was a knock on the glass door bearing the name of my company, 'APE'. Not waiting for my response, a tall well-groomed woman entered and promptly sat in the chair opposite me.

"You are the proprietor I believe," she asked. "So, I'll get down to business straight away. My daughter is having an affair with a most unspeakable character whom I want dealt with." She paused for a moment, "How much"?

"All depends," I replied. "On what you propose."

"Just for him to be gone out of my daughter's life, if you know what I mean," she answered with a sideways look. I asked her for the name of this unsuitable character and was astounded to hear my name.

Of course, her daughter did not have a photograph of me as in my line of business photographs and names are not readily given.

"No problem, madam, I shall see to it at once."

The air was a lot cleaner after she left and took her overbearing perfume with her.

Later I straightened the room and closed the door on that part of my life for good and met up for a stroll along the Bayou. Explaining what had happened that afternoon and the plans I had for us to recreate our lives elsewhere the agreement came readily.

The envelope posted in the state we chose to live contained the letter:

Mother,

I have started a better life with the one I truly love.

Oh! And by the way the man you spoke to in the office of A.P.E hasn't got out of my life as you suggested.

We have joined forces in the hope of finding a better life together. It was not our intention to make a monkey out of you, but 'All Problems Eliminated'! The problem wasn't solved it was Eliminated for all of us!

Season of Dreams by Annette Pickering

I walk the path that once was wet,
Now cracked like dry savannah plains.
The furrows hard beneath my feet,
Wait open mouthed for summer rains.

The heady haze of new mown hay,
Hangs languid in the evening air.
The midges dance their merry dance,
They heed no person walking there.

The hedgerows either side of me
Are flush with undeveloped fruit.
But soon the autumn will bring forth,
A startling change along my route

The trees that stand so strong and tall,
Their leafy boughs all decked in green.
Too soon will change to golden brown,
Before their nakedness is seen.

The seasons changing day by day,
The berries ripen red and black.
And with this metamorphosis,
I know there is no turning back.

And when the winter is in sight,
All gone the greens and golden brown.
The colours vanish overnight,
Beneath a snowy eiderdown.

So, with these thoughts, I amble on.
The seasons changing in my mind.
As life's full circle follows on,
I'll leave the past behind.

Limerick by Jo Bennett

My dog and my cat had a fight.
It happened late last Monday night.
She screeched and he growled,
And the neighbours all scowled.
Now I daren't leave them out of my sight!

The Return by Linda Scholes

Mary was dozing in the wooden armchair by the fire, a pair of socks she was darning, resting on her knee, when there was a gentle knock at the door.

Late to be calling, she thought, as she would normally have been in bed. The working day at the mill was a long one and, these days, Mary felt all her sixty years. She opened the door and peered out into the misty night. Thick fog had descended, as it often did in this industrial town. A figure emerged from out of the gloom. Shocked, Mary realised it was her son, Jack, missing these five years. His face was thin and gaunt, his eyes downcast.

"Mam, I will understand if you don't want me to stay. I've been walking for days to get here. If I could just rest a while and then I'll be on my way."

Mary didn't hesitate, opening the door wide, she put her arms around her son and drew him towards the warmth of the fire. "It's good to see you. I'll make us a cup of tea. Are you hungry? I have a bit of fruit cake your grannie's made."

"That would be champion, Mam."

When Mary returned with a tray, Jack was asleep. She eased his worn boots off his feet, noting how threadbare his socks were and covered him with her shawl.

A weight lifted from her shoulders. Mary climbed the stairs to bed knowing her boy was safe and, she hoped, back where he belonged.

Keeping the child alive by Caroline Bradley

Helter-Skelter, Etch-a-Sketch,
Spirograph, ludo & chess,
These childhood names, they take me back
To carefree days
In my ever-distant past.
I whiled away long playful hours,
The passing of time forgotten in
Muddy puddles, sniffing flowers.
I would carelessly drift between reality & fantasy,
One moment me, the next someone else,
A princess, bionic woman, action man,
Living the life that might once be mine...
Or not.
Gameshows & talent shows
New Faces, Bullseye, The Golden Shot
Peppered my past times with fun & prizes,
Marking my time through
Daily shows & weekly slots,
The sun always setting & the moon always rising.
I grew up with these things
Each year getting taller & wiser,
My memory bank getting fuller & fuller.
I thought it might burst...
That would be a first...
But it mostly just shifted,
Some moments far forward, some back in reverse.
I remember the feelings, the smells & the taste,
The preciousness of teddies, the busyness of fetes,
Those days of wonder opening my eyes
With what I saw, felt & learned,
Every day a surprise

Waiting for me to find.
I sometimes think I wouldn't mind
Going back to those days.
Sometimes they feel close
Sometimes far, far away,
But I know they all made me,
The things of my past,
My memories are special
And I hope they will last.

Humpty Dumpty by Jayne Fallows

The Queen was doing a reality show in the jungle and the King was in the Big Brother house. The King's army were bored. They had nothing to do. No one to guard. The Captain of the Guard decided he had to find something to do so he contacted Human Resources and arranged to go on a health and safety course.

Several days later he went to see Humpty Dumpty.

"What do you want?" said Humpty, balancing precariously on one leg on top of the wall.

"I have good news," said the captain. "After generations of Dumpty's falling off that wall, I now know how to stop it because I've done a risk assessment and I'm here to keep you safe."

"Hmmm," said Humpty, moving gracefully into a handstand.

"Stop!" said the captain, putting his hands out in a catching position. "You are in great danger. If you fall, you'll break, and no-one knows how to put you back together again."

"I've been on a course too," said Humpty proudly. "Circus Skills! The terms of my ASBO said I had to do something useful with my time and learn a new skill. So, I chose Circus Skills. Look!"

He flipped over in a double somersault and landed on one hand.

"You have to stop," said the captain. "There are serious health and safety issues at stake. Humpty, don't be a numpty, listen to me."

"YOU CAN'T STOP ME." Humpty shouted. "If you do it's a breach of my human rights. I have the right to do my tricks on any wall I choose. I've learned all the skills I need."

"I urge you to reconsider, "said the captain. "If you fall off, think of the mess. It will pose a serious slip hazard to the public. I'll have to get my men to cone off the whole area.

"What about some protective clothing," he continued. "Then if you fall, you'll be unharmed? We could lower the height of the wall or put a protective fence around the top. I'm open to negotiations."

"I'm not wearing a shell suit," said Humpty. "I have my image to think about. The Paparazzi could take my photograph at any time. I'm bringing out a new range of tableware next month. I can't be seen wearing just anything."

The course hadn't prepared the captain for such resistance. What should he do? How could he sleep at night knowing that one of their most famous citizens was putting himself in such danger?

He decided to have another go the next day. Perhaps more pleading would do the trick.

When he arrived at the wall Humpty was nowhere to be seen. The captain breathed a sigh of relief. Humpty had seen sense. What a result!

Then he heard movement behind him. It was Humpty. "I'm so glad you've seen sense," said the captain. "I've been so worried about you."

"Well, not exactly," said Humpty. "My agent called. I've had an offer I can't refuse. I'm going to appear on MasterChef next week. Apparently, they think I could make the perfect omelette!"

By the River by Jo Bennett

Right – I didn't push Bigsy in the river. He was messing about with my stuff and just trying to get on my nerves, so I went to whack him, and he dodged out of the way. He just slipped – it was so muddy he slipped and just slid right down the bank and into the water. He went right under!

Me and Daz went to the edge but couldn't get near enough to see anything. We tried leaning further over and then Daz fell in as well! I was yelling and shouting, and a man came – he must have been fishing further up the bank. He just ripped his jacket off and jumped straight in the river. He sort of shoved Daz up the bank and I yanked him up onto the grass.

Then he went back for Bigsy who had floated up a bit further out. He pulled him over to the edge and we somehow got him up out of the water. He looked awful – all covered in grey mud and slime, and he just lay there. The man turned him over and sort of thumped him. Then he started pushing and pushing him. I just didn't know what to do.

Suddenly Bigsy coughed and spluttered a bit and then he just moaned. The man said he would need an ambulance. He got a phone out of his jacket and rang for one. When the ambulance men came, they said he needed to get to hospital, so they put him on a stretcher.

By then Daz was shivering and nearly starting to cry so I gave him my jumper. He was soaking wet and muddy, but I didn't really like that jumper anyway. Then we all got to ride in the ambulance, which was a bit neat. On the way they kept doing things to Bigsy but said that he should be ok.

When we got to the hospital, we had to give all our names and addresses to the nurse. Next thing everybody turned up - Bigsy's mum and dad, Daz's big sister and my mum. They were all talking at once.

Mum gave me a real shouting at. Then the next thing, she started kissing and hugging me in front of everybody – which was even worse!

Bisgy's going to be all right but now, but we've been told that we can't go down by the river ever again – which is a bit tight.

Still, they might change their minds again later, you never know. Parents are weird like that.

Lockdown Life: Rainbow by Caroline Bradley

I love a good rainbow.
By that I mean a full crock of gold to crock of gold umbra,
Arcing and arching across the open sky, offering a full spectrum of hope and possibilities.
An after-the-rain, lift your heads and hearts up to the heavens, expanse of colour,
All the colours, the many technicolour colours of dreams and dreamcoats.
Where will it take us this rainbow, while we're locked up and locked down,
With our little escapes, here and there, but not too many and not too far,
Masked and unmasked, like fans at a comic convention
Expressing our inner superhero but not sure what the dress-code is anymore.
Conventional or unconventional, what is right or wrong, safe or unsafe.
The rainbow arches over all of this confusion and conundrum,
Protecting and promising that after the rain
There will be sunlight.

Duty by Linda Scholes

Edward felt his stomach churning and turning over and over. He tried to conceal the shaking of his body from his fellow soldiers as he waited, his boots submerged in the muddy water that filled the trench, for the commence to 'go over the top.'

He wasn't brave, he was frightened. He only joined up because his best friend, Albert persuaded him. They were only sixteen. Their send-off was glorious, marching through the town with the bands playing, the crowd cheering – off to fight for King and country. It was to be an adventure.

Nothing had prepared him for the reality of war. Most of the time, he felt so scared he just wanted to run away but the penalty for desertion was a death sentence and, so he continued to play the part of the patriotic soldier.

Albert was killed in action the week they arrived. The weather had been bad for days, the sleet and rain relentlessly poured down. Out on the battlefield, the conditions were awful. One minute Albert was running along next to Edward as they headed towards the enemy line, the next he was gone, killed by a sniper's bullet.

Edward dived into a shell hole and stayed there clutching his rifle to his chest, until he heard the shout to retreat. He couldn't believe he made it back without a scratch.

He missed Albert. He missed his mother and sister.

The order came. He pushed his reluctant body up the ladder, weapon at the ready to charge blindly through a field of fire. He knew what he had to do. He knew he had no choice.

There's a Hole in My School shoes by Rob Tuson

There's a hole in my school shoes,
my school shoes,
my school shoes,
there's a hole in my school shoes oh what should I do.

Replace them with new ones,
with new ones,
with new ones,
replace them with new ones that's what you should do.

But, there's a virus
dear Liza,
dear Liza,
dear Liza,
there's a virus dear Liza I can't leave the house.

Log on to a website
and get them delivered,
log on to a website they'll be with you soon.

My laptop's stopped working,
stopped working,
stopped working,
my laptop's stopped working, I'm totally stuffed.

Here use my old iPhone,
old iPhone,
old iPhone,
here use my old iPhone it gets you on-line.

I don't know your passcode,
your passcode,
your passcode,
I don't know your passcode oh GDPR.

It's unlocked and ready
and ready
and ready,
it's unlocked and ready, now here's a great pair.

But they won't come till Friday,
till Friday,
till Friday,
they won't come till Friday, I need them right now.

Well click and collect them,
collect them,
collect them,
well click, and collect them from their Cheadle store.

But there's a virus dear Liza,
dear Liza,
dear Liza,
there's a virus dear Liza, I can't leave the house.

Rapunzel in Lockdown by Jenny

My name is Rapunzel and I live in the Ivory Towers, New Forest. I have the penthouse suite and very nice it is too. Usually, I'm happy with my own company for short periods but since the lock down started, I've found it very lonely with only the telly for company and even that's on the blink now.

I really miss my lovely friend, Snow White. She's a laugh a minute with her stories about the little folk she lives with. She won't be lonely during this lockdown because she's part of an extended bubble with the dwarfs, but I suspect they'll be driving her up the wall by now, especially that Grumpy.

I'd even appreciate a visit from the old witch who imprisoned me up here in the first place, only she's clinically vulnerable and has to self-isolate for the foreseeable future.

Do you know, I haven't had a single suitor calling to me, "Rapunzel, Rapunzel, let down your hair," since January.

My hair was very long before, but you should see it now, I haven't been to the hairdressers for months. What's that song?

All I want is someone some where
To come and wash and style my hair
In one enormous chair
Oh, wouldn't it be loverley, loverley.

It takes me ages to wash it and it's so thick I have to hang out of the window to dry it. It takes all day and I get insects and butterflies caught. The other day a bird flew in and got tangled.

Poor me!

But hang on, who's that driving up in his van? A nice young man, and he's got some very long ladders. Perhaps he's another suitor, or maybe he's just come to fix my telly.

Limerick by Jo Bennett

There was a young lady called Alice.
Who wanted to live in a palace.
She became so affected
Her friends all defected.
But it wasn't just done out of malice.

Ben to the Rescue by Jenny

My gran lives on a remote island off the coast of Ireland, and I get to spend all summer with her while Mum and Dad go off on their explorations. It's a bit of a tortuous journey but the sea is calm, and Gran is there to meet me on the quay. She wraps her big arms around me, and I smell her usual lavender perfume.

"I've got a special present for you this holiday, Ben. But right now, let's get up to the cottage you must be so hungry."

"What's my present Gran, I can't wait to find out."

"Well," she said slowly, "how would you like to be able to transport yourself anywhere in the world? Where would you go, what would you do?"

"What? How?" I spluttered. "I don't understand how that could work and how you can organise that?"

"I have a few contacts and favours to call in." she hinted mysteriously, "and I thought it would be useful to keep you entertained this summer".

She handed me a small black box.

"Well, I'd love to see what Mum and Dad are up to; they are somewhere in Egypt excavating an ancient tomb with the authorities. It's all hush hush though. Can I pinpoint their exact location?"

"You can do anything and go anywhere you like, but remember, you only have a few hours to play with each time. Bit like Cinderella eh," she chuckled.

"Go on, no time to waste - just say – 'Beam me up Scotty' and you're off."

Next thing I'm outside a tiny opening in a sun-baked rock and I know I have to go through that gap. It's claustrophobic and dark as I enter. Bending low I follow the passage deep into the cliff. I can hear raised voices, and recognise my dad saying, "You're robbing your own people of their heritage. Just let us go and we'll keep quiet".

"Too late, Professor Lyons, we've got clients waiting to pay top price for these items. You are just hindrances now, and alas, in the way. So, goodbye."

"Beam me up Scotty," I whisper and find myself in the baking heat outside near the helicopter, which is ready for take-off, the pilot leaning nonchalantly against the open door, waiting. I creep up and grab the ignition keys.

"Beam me up Scotty" I whisper again.

In no time I am able to alert the Egyptian authorities to the theft and guide them into the hidden valley where the thieves are frantically searching the helicopter for the keys and screaming at the pilot. I rush into the tiny opening to find my parents tied up and exhausted.

"Ben, my lad, don't know how you've got here but thank heavens for your quick reactions in stopping those tomb raiders. Well done, son. I guess there'll be a reward for you but how on earth did you find us?"

I explained about Gran and her fantastic gift. Dad laughed. "I always thought she had a hot line to the leprechauns, and this proves it."

Limerick by Glenda Davies

A lazy young farmer named Fred
Refused to get up from his bed
Mother gave him a clout
As she booted him out
Now he sleeps in the hayloft instead

I Write This Sitting in the Sink by Annette Pickering

Why are you sitting in the sink? I hear you ask.

Well, it all started with himself wanting a carrot cake. I'm not one for baking, but thought I'd give it a go.

The rarely used recipe book was on the top shelf of the cupboard. So, I fetched the step stool from under the stairs. As I reached up, I knocked the ketchup of the shelf. Of course, it was a glass bottle because I'm doing my bit for the environment.

Ketchup laced with fine slithers of glass spread like molten butter across the kitchen floor. I cursed silently. He always said the ketchup should be kept in the fridge, but the bottle was too tall.

Down on my knees, I tried carefully to scrape up the mess so I could clean the floor. Even that would have to be done by hand because I'd forgotten to replace the broken mop.

Working my way backwards from the doorway to the sink, the floor slowly returned to its usual pristine state.

As usual, something else I've done wrong, I thought as I climbed onto the sink to wait for the floor to dry.

Well, if he wants carrot cake, he'll have to go and buy one.

It's the whole truth by Estelle Weiner

It failed. The M O T.
Shock - no not me, the absorber.
Just one shock absorber.
Must be those pot holes.

Agreed.

Oh well, better replace them both. Sod's law, you do just one, then the
other goes.

Agreed.

Pot holes? I ask myself - where's the **pot** and what exactly is a **hole**?
In fact, a hole is just a state of nothing.
The absence of .... what?
An empty space.
For a word that actually means the absence of matter, it is used in an
inordinately, almost unreasonable, number of ways.

Sometimes they make sense. We have **sink holes, plug holes,
blackholes**. A **hole in one** is to be applauded.

It can get very personal as well. And not always complimentary.
Mostly to do with the part of us that holds our brain box.
A **hole in the head** is a tad derogatory after all, but then we have **lug
holes** or more politely, **ear holes**.

Strangely our nose holes have the more esoteric name of nostrils. That
stems from the old English word nosthyrle being two words actually.
Nosu for nose and thyrel - yes you guessed it, hole. And all these are
situated above your **cakehole**.

Unless you are an American. They may ask you to shut your **pie hole**. And as for your eyes, well they could be used to look through a **spy hole, a peephole,** and of course, a **keyhole.**

Further down the physical structure known as our body, we will find perhaps a **buttonhole**, and if you get as far as your arms, you can **dig yourself into a hole.**

Moving away from the obsession with our body, we can visit a **watering hole**, where if they serve food as well as drink, we can order **toad in the hole**.

Unsurprisingly, no cookbook sleuth can determine where the toad came from. Some think it's the similarity to the required piece of meat peeping out of the batter, ready to jump on its prey.

Something you then might be persuaded to put down your **cakehole.**

Funny the names we have for food- **Bubble and Squeak, Spotted Dick.** I'm sure there are plenty more, but I'll leave that to you to play games with.

As for me, I need to pay for those shock absorbers. I'm off to find a **hole in the wall.**

Fresh Poem by Maggie Waker

Here's a good value freshly baked poem
Not a cup cake.
Which are only fairy cakes without wings.
Maybe twice the size but twelve times the price

Recipe for a Carer's Dream by Annette Pickering

Take 30 seconds from a thunderclap.
Add a ten-second flash of lightning.
A pot of gold to catch the rainbow after the storm.
A bucket full of tears, to wash away the pain.
A handful of tender touch and all will be healed.
A wondrous hug from gentle arms.
To catch you when you fall.
Miles of smiles to help you through your troubles.
With lots of rainbow coloured bubbles to send them on their way.

Caring (Being a Carer) by a Carer

Everyone cares for different things in different ways
And as my mum's gaze alights upon my face
My heart soars – today is a good day

I care for my mum in her dementia years as I would my child
We lie together on the bed
I stroke her forehead
Tell her stories and bring her news
And I am honoured to do so

I help her to dress and coax her to eat
And massage her feet
And I am honoured to do so

But now I'm in the world of care home fees
And selling the family home
Whilst my mum sits alone
In an unfamiliar room

I feel in turn
Relieved, angry, guilty, afraid
Is this the right decision I made?

Now strangers look after my mum
Whilst I haunt the home – checking, listening, monitoring
Asking questions of the staff
I feel frightened to do so

My visits are lengthy but full of laughter and tears
As we reminisce about the years gone by
The people and places she knew
This I am honoured to do

For a brief time, she is the mother
And I am the child
She worries and frets
And gets upset

When she asks if her house has been sold
And I lie and say no
It hurts me to do so

We look through her memory box together
But her gaze slips away
As she cries
Do I go home today?

The end comes with a stroke
Which takes her mind but not her breath
She breathes on for three long days
She is strong – my mum

I gaze at my mum's lovely face
As I wipe away her tears
And the years slip away
I am once again the child
Lost without my mum

Now four years on
The "What if's" and "if only's" still
Flood my mind
People are kind to reassure
That 'you couldn't have done anything more'
But I'm not so sure

Only my mum has the answer …

Love at First Sight by Anne Hammond

From the first time I set eyes on Jack it was love at first sight. I really had no intention of bringing another dog into my life at that time. It was eight years ago, and we had a ten-year-old border collie Ollie who was enjoying becoming a spoilt premature older (only) dog. Also, Neil my late husband was in bad health, and it would be me looking after and training another puppy.

However, it was one wintry February night when our daughter Zoe burst in the front door with a big smile on her face. She had her winter coat zipped up to her chin and peeping out at the top was the cutest white fluffy puppy with big brown eyes and brown pricked up ears. He was a collie crossed with a quarter husky. That puppy was Jack.

From that moment my resolve not to bring another puppy in the house vanished. I was hooked and so was Neil. Zoe, yet again, had wound us both round her little finger. Apparently little Jack had been headed for GUMTREE. Zoe's friend had got Jack on a whim and had soon tired of him. Zoe who is a dog lover was expecting her second baby and already had a dog and cat of her own or she would have had him in a flash.

Well, I have never had one day of regret letting that cute puppy into our lives. Our older dog Ollie had a new lease of life and they got on great. Jack, learning how to behave from his elder mature 'brother'.

Having Jack was great for Neil and in the next two or three years he was able to enjoy him. It was about that time our little collie Ollie passed away and we were left with Jack who by that time had become my beautiful, faithful, dependable, companion.

Neil's health was now very poor, and I didn't notice that I had become his 'carer'. It was a gradual process, and it took a couple of years for me to accept that fact. My life was very different now. I retired from work, a position I had had for 28 happy years, working for

40

Stockport's Vernon Building Society with a wonderful set of friends and colleagues. We were like a big family. Very happy years. However, becoming a full-time carer made it impossible to carry on doing both.

So, over the next few years it was having Jack that got me through those tough times looking after Neil. He is always at my side and our daily walks are the highlight of both our lives usually twice a day. Every time I put my coat on, he is at the front door ready to go out. There is no leaving him behind.

Having a dog is a great way of meeting people and making friends and that's exactly what happened to me. Never a day goes by without seeing someone to chat and pass the time of day with. Jack looks forward to meeting his doggy friends and has one very special girlfriend.

Sadly, Neil passed away in September 2020 and it's a very different life we have now. It's not just me that is grieving, Jack is as well. We are a twosome and that's a fact.

Limerick by Jo Bennett

A very old man, name of Fred,
He one night fell out of his bed.
He lay on the floor,
Fairly close to the door.
Then decided to bunk there instead.

JABBERCOVIDCHOCKY by Caroline Bradley

I've had the jab,
It wasn't bad,
Just a prick in the arm,
In a speck of time,
From an efficient nurse
With a reassuring smile on her face
And a sharp needle
In her steady hand.
I've been here before
In days of yore.
TB, Rubella, Typhoid & the like,
Each making my life that bit
Safer & more protected.
And as a Mum,
Holding my babes tight
For the needle that could
One day
Save their Life.

Blu Tac Scars by Jo Bennett

My very own place, those first student digs,
We all felt like kings, though we lived more like pigs!
That very first room, I remember so well,
the end of range colours - the mysterious smell.
All the walls were a mess, but it didn't matter
Good old Blu Tac and posters hid most of the tatter.
A house full of strangers became such close friends.
We'd argue and curse but then make amends.
We felt like pioneers - independent, alone.
But that soon wore thin once the money was gone!
Eating beans every day seems fun looking back.
When the treat of the week was just a Big Mac.
So, we nicked a few signs and we pinched a few cones.
I lost so much weight you could see all my bones!
We acted the fool and sailed close to the law,
But just being young was our only real flaw.
And we all fell in love, though we'd sworn that we wouldn't
But the girls were so great, resist them we couldn't!
We each had our heartbreaks, supported each other.
And cured them with drink and the aid of a brother.
We threw-up in phone boxes, cafes and bars,
The cream of the crop – oh yeah, we were real stars!
Then – who said exams? That was serious stuff.
How much time is there left? Hell, my notes are just rough!
Did I miss that lecture? So, who's got the book?
Hey, do you understand this? Let's just have a look.
And we all knuckled down, the high life soon pale.
We sweated with fear when we thought that we'd failed.
We started to pack, and the bin bags were filled.
We attempted to clean where the curries had spilled.
All the posters came down, but the Blu Tac just stayed!

Would we get our deposit back? We quietly prayed!
Well, some of us shone - and some just survived
But we'd gained such a lot since the day we arrived.
We'd learned much together, foundations were laid.
………..………. and those Blu Tac scars will never fade.

Coincidences by Jean H

Life is full of coincidences it is said, and I seem to have more than my fair share. Last night I watched a programme about the author of Dr Zhivago. Later on, doing a crossword a question was, "Who wrote Dr Zhivago?" Coincidence maybe, but these happenings come every few months in clusters. So, it was no surprise that the following day there occurred another one.

It had been a particularly trying morning and my spirits were rather low with one thing and another. But I knew I had to get through the day and shop for the lunch later on. There was a light drizzle, which does not make it easy for walking at my age, but I put on my stout shoes and proceeded to get my thoughts into gear as to what to get for lunch.

Bag, handbag plus the skimpiest of shopping list I set forth for the walk to the shops. Walking up the slight rise I came to the school I used to attend but was mindful of the kerb that was and still is a tripping hazard. Negotiating myself over the problem area with care I happened to glance up and noticed some-one looking at me. My first thought was 'Oh no, what now?''

Hello, don't you recognise me?

No, why should I?

You used to be ...

I still am! I made to walk past but the stranger persisted.

We attended this school a long time ago.

AND? I was beginning to get a little bit annoyed by now.

The kerb you have just so carefully avoided tripping on was the one I fell over coming home from school that one day.

My brain was trying hard to remember this incident but to no avail.

You were the one who came to my assistance when all around just laughed.I had to have quite a lot of dental work done to repair the damage that day. I have never forgotten the kindness you showed me,

46

and it has stayed with me all these years. You showed me the way by being kind to others and I have followed your way ever since then. But I did forget to say, 'Thank You'.

Vaguely through the mists of time I did remember but had put the occasion out of my mind as it was just a normal reaction to a situation.

I am so glad to have the opportunity to see you again and thank you for showing me the way.

I nodded and proceeded on my quest to get the groceries.

On my return home from the shopping trip, I came to that 'kerb' again and remembered I had not replied but had just nodded. How very rude of me.

Then drinking my morning coffee, I got to wondering about my coincidences. KERB was shouting in my thoughts.... was this another coincidence? I seem to remember after the encounter this morning, glancing backwards there was no-one there.

Welcome to the World by Jo Bennett

So, welcome to the world little man.
It seems I've been entrusted with your care.
I wonder what you will become,
What might you achieve?
I sense a beauty in you already and
I must not damage that precious soul!
I will simply stand guard for a while,
Until you are strong enough to stand alone.
If I can just allow you to grow,
Not damage what is already there
And not impose myself on you,
Who knows what you might be?
……. forgive me if I make mistakes

Limerick by Jo Bennett

My pet is as big as a house.
I thought she would just catch the mouse.
She blundered around,
Made a terrible sound.
And the ruin she left is MY HOUSE!

Glass Slippers by Rob Tuson

With the benefit of hindsight signing up for an online dating account probably wasn't the smartest move. I'd realised the marriage was doomed from our wedding night. My friends used to say to me, how can a relationship between a downtrodden and put upon, yet stunningly beautiful, skivvy and an eligible handsome future king work.

It was just so tedious in the royal household. You couldn't lift a finger to do the simplest of tasks. Even a sneeze would be met with a proffered handkerchief. Prince Charming, it had also turned out, was more Prince Boring. The honeymoon was just that – a honeymoon period, swiftly followed by one tedious public engagement after another and whilst his highness mixed with the movers and shakers of The Kingdom, your lowness here was reduced to vacuous smiles, handshakes, and small talk with the housewives of the Enchanted City.

Kevin was astonished when my online dating profile proved to be the only accurate one on the whole site. When I said he'd be getting his own little princess to love and cherish I wasn't joking. Kevin is no reconstructed man or metrosexual male, but he knows how to treat me and respect me and if I have a nostalgic urge to shovel some coal into a grate he knows not to stand in my way.

Monogamy it seems is vitally important to the Palace, Glass slippers don't fetch as much on eBay as you might expect, especially when they have chips in the heels the size of the ones on Prince Charming's shoulders. But nonetheless we scraped enough together for a security deposit and Kevin and I set up home, in a compact four bed semi well away from the prying eyes of the palace.

At first, I was reluctant to allow Kevin's widowed mum and two divorced sisters to share the house with us. Once bitten, twice shy, but they can't afford the local property prices and quite frankly they have nowhere else to go. They are refreshingly appreciative of my culinary skills and housekeeping expertise. In return my mother-in-law is my bingo partner on a Tuesday night and my sisters-in-law are great company on our shopping trips to the local outlet mall.

Furthermore, it appears that we will be soon having a bawl. I'm not showing yet and given the dates we might need a DNA test, but we are expecting a male heir to the throne, who will be the best cared for and loved little prince in the whole kingdom, with live in babysitters to boot.

My advice is therefore to be careful what you wish for. The grass isn't always greener, and fantasies should remain just that; something elusive and completely unattainable.

However bleak your situation may appear, there are always positive aspects to be drawn from and built upon. A job well done for someone who appreciates it is far more valuable and rewarding than an expensive welcome present in return for a wave in a gloved hand.

From Another Point of View by Annette Pickering

Grumpy was always grumpy. Hence the name. Firstly, he was fed up with going to work every day, then coming home to the overcrowded house in the middle of nowhere.

Grumpy longed for a different life.

He'd heard there was a place with beautiful piles of golden sand, called beaches. These were next to a giant eternal lake where waves rolled gently in and out in a soothing peaceful motion. The digging there would be so much easier in the soft sand than in the darkness of the deep dark mines he endured every day.

And now, they were even more overcrowded. This person, they called a girl had moved in.

What sort of a creature was she? Tall and slender with extremely long legs and wearing brightly coloured clothes. Even worse, she was always singing. When what he wanted was peace and quiet and time to be miserable on his own.

This girl kept moving things around so he couldn't find them. "Where's my socks?" he grumbled. The giant creature smiled sweetly at him as she handed him the freshly laundered items.

It's not good this, it's not good at all. He thought to himself. I have to leave. I have to get away from here.

OR get rid of HER.

When I grow old by Estelle Weiner

Age is just a number
Getting old is a state of being
A state of being hidden in the cloak of time

Age is a period in time
Science will blind us with numbers
Numbers we find hard to understand

To understand the numbers
To understand their meaning
You first have to understand yourself

If I were young by Jenny

If I were young and fancy free
I'd buy a camper van
With tins and tetra packs of milk
I'd set off North -
Just my dog, Shep, and me.
We'd drive for miles, and miles and miles
And reach the furthest point
Of Scotland, then take a ferry ride
To some distant lonely isle,
Just my dog, Shep, and me.

I'd never shave, just skinny dip
In streams of crystal water,
I'd fish for trout and walk and climb
And follow forest tracks and trust to luck
We'd make it back
In time to sit and watch the sun go down.
Just my dog, Shep, and me.

A time to think and plan my life
Glad to be fit and free
A time of peace, a time of rest
And as the million trillion stars come out,
They'd fill the sky, and
I would know
That I am truly blessed,
With my old dog, Shep, and me.

Now that I'm older and fancy free
I'll buy that camper van and travel North
To Scotland for that ferry ride

To my enchanted isle.
We'll find my loch and glass in hand,
We'll toast our good luck and, as planned,
We'll enjoy our stay,
(But not skinny dip!)
My dear wife, Morag, and me.

Gower Hall by Linda Scholes

It was wartime and Sylvia's girls' school had been evacuated to Gower Hall, an Elizabethan mansion in the Shropshire countryside. She enjoyed the historic atmosphere of the old place and loved the paintings of past inhabitants that lined the walls, their eyes seeming to follow her when she walked by them.

She especially loved exploring and discovering secret places the other girls didn't know about. She rather liked to be alone sometimes, so would often slip away and hide.

After supper she climbed the staircase to the attic, took off her blazer, threw her school tie into the corner and spread a blanket out on the floor. She sat down, lit a candle, placed it on the hearth and took a book out of her school bag.

Earlier, she had managed to slip into the library with its floor to ceiling extensive collection of books. It was strictly off limits to the girls but Sylvia though it was worth risking punishment just to handle those ancient tomes and even to borrow one.

She cradled the large leather-bound book, tracing the lettering on its ornately decorated covering, "Stories of Ghostly Hauntings". With care, she opened it and traced her finger down the list of chapter headings until she found "Chapter VIII, Gower Hall" and, at the appropriate page read:

'Gower Hall is primarily known for the ghosts of two of the previous occupants, Lord John Gower and his wife, Priscilla. Lord John was found dead in the attic one evening having suffered a seizure.

He was interested in studying the stars, which were visible through the window in the roof.

Two days later, his wife, Lady Priscilla also died suddenly, it was said of a broken heart.

There are reported sightings of a lady dressed in white who, when the moon is full, materializes at the entrance to the attic and raps on the door, the noise can be heard in the rooms below. She then

*appears to pass through the wall and enters the attic room,
presumably looking for her beloved John.'*

It was as Sylvia read this line that she heard knocking echoing across the room.

Fearfully she looked towards the door ...

Limerick by Jo Bennett

She ate a huge plateful of jelly.
It caused dreadful pains in her belly.
She moaned and she cried,
and she thought she had died.
Then later just sat and watched telly.

Limerick by Glenda Davies

Last week Winnie proudly announced
She had purchased a sweet little mouse
Not content with his cheeses
Mouse eats what he pleases
Now mouse is as big as a house

Loser by Jayne Fallows

He barely lifted his head as his wife put the mug of steaming tea next to him. He was too deep in thought to even notice her. She broke the silence first, "It's happened again, hasn't it?"

She had managed to squeeze most of the water from his clothes, but huge drips splashed onto the floor as they hung to dry next to the fire. She wasn't sure how much more of this he could take. The stress was starting to affect his health. Constant headaches, chest pains and sleepless nights were really taking it out of him.

The Doctor had said, "Perhaps you should consider a change of career."

"I won't be beaten," he'd told the Doctor. But, in truth a change of career wasn't going to be easy. He had limited skills, having worked in the same job for as long as he could remember. How else could he earn a living?

He shifted in his seat and shivered. "Come on, my dear, drink your tea. It will help to warm you through," said his wife.

He picked up the mug and took a long swig and then putting his head in his hands began to cry. "Why are they being so mean to me? Day after day I try to communicate with them. Try to do my job properly. Why can't they be nice to me?"

"You need a break," said his wife. "Perhaps a short holiday would help?"

"How can we afford that?" he wailed. "I've had my wages docked every month this year because of them. We're in debt up to my whiskers, behind with the rent, the cart has been re-possessed and now it looks as though I'll lose my job altogether."

"Perhaps a few days off work would make you feel better," she said.

"No. I have to face them one more time. I must. Just one last try, and if that doesn't work I will pack the job in. I suppose we'll manage somehow. I could always get a job in a call centre."

His wife looked worried. "Do you want to talk about what happened today?"

"I got there before them, and I was feeling really positive. Then, they arrived – laughing and jeering at me as usual. I ignored them, like you told me to, but then I realised that one of them was carrying a sign. At first, I couldn't make out the words, but as they got closer it became clear just what they were getting at.

"Then, they changed tactics. Usually, the two smaller ones come first followed by the biggest one. Well, today the big one came first."

"I'm coming past you little man," he said. "If you try to stop me you know what will happen." So, I told him, 'Look, I've got a job to do. It's not personal. I must do this, or I will lose my job.' He refused of course. He told me to step aside or else ..."

His wife looked concerned. "Or else what?" she said.

"He didn't say, but I was really scared. He moved towards me with his head bowed and then he just knocked me into the water like before. The rest you know."

"Did you say anything to upset him?" said his wife.

"Only the usual, 'Who's that trip trapping over my bridge?' Sometimes I add fol di rol just to lighten the mood, but I didn't even say that today."

"Oh, you poor dear," she said. "But you never told me what the sign said."

"It said – 'Latest score: Goats 10 Troll zero."

Mindful Mess by Caroline Bradley

Peace of mind
Is hard to find
In a pandemic.
It paces around
Trying to ground itself
In ever-changing times.
It drags its knuckles along the floor
Shooting sparks
And shaking your
Calmness into fright,
Taking flight your
Feelings of security
And peace.
I'm trying to recreate
Soothing thoughts
Through the ache
Of what's missing
And gone.
When the world is so wrong
How can I feel right?
But I know I must
Keep on being strong
And looking for the light.

Memories of Home by Arthur Spedding

I can remember my mum having a mangle to wring out water from our clothes after she had washed them by hand in the kitchen sink at our home in Reddish. We had that mangle for a few years until we could eventually afford a washing machine.

My mum used to warn me and my two sisters to be careful not to put our fingers anywhere near the mangle or we would lose them. As far as I can remember the mangle was by the side of the kitchen sink until some time in the early 60's and it was used two or three times a week and always on a Monday, which was wash day.

I saw one recently on one of the television antique shows so it was the first thing that came to mind when I was asked to write about something from the past that today's children probably would not know about. I doubt whether any of our grandchildren or any of our own grown-up children would know what a mangle was or how it worked.

I think the one we had at home eventually broke which would have been when we first bought our first automatic washing machine.

I don't remember my dad ever using the mangle.

Stone Soup by Jean H

The bent figure passed through the town walls walking slowly with his burden of a pan and bedding roll into the town square where he would find shelter and safety from the thieves and robbers of the countryside who, like him, were hungry and cold.

Finding a spot near the town hall wall he settled down with his meagre belongings, placing his precious pan close by so he was able to keep his eye and hand on it. The weather was closing in, and the heat of the afternoon sun was weakening. He was only one of many people seeking sanctuary that night. Turning his attention to the coming night he placed his bedding roll on the ground, and he lay down covering himself with the cloak from his shoulders.

The night was long and cold but lying next to the wall it did give some shred of comfort which dwindled as morning came and with it a sharp frost which lay heavily on his cloak. Reminding himself to get prepared for the day ahead he shuffled out from under his rime covered covering. Crossing to the communal water pump he put in just the right amount of water in the pan and carried it back to his place in the town square. Taking some wood from his back carrier he lit a small fire and on it placed the pan with the water on the fire. He then proceeded to take a stone out of his pocket which he placed in the pan.

This aroused the curiosity of people who were just becoming awake and wondered over to the fire to see what was happening. One by one he was asked what he was doing with a stone in a pan? "It's Stone Soup," he answered.

"What is the purpose of that then?" came yet another question.

"It's all I have. I invite you to place anything edible you have to put in the pan along with the stone."

People brought the food they wished to place in the pan along with the stone. When all had been cooking for about an hour, another invitation came, "If you bring your spoons and bowl, we will soon have a feast."

All those who contributed to the pan soon returned with spoons and bowls and the contents of the pan was shared out between the participants. Leaving some left in the pan for himself (but not eating the stone) the traveller enjoyed the soup which was made very tasty by all the different ingredients. Everyone felt better after the meal and the morning didn't seem quite as cold as it had been earlier on. Packing up his belongings and after washing the soup pan at the pump he walked back through the town gates on his way to the next town.

The stone? That was kept very safe for the next time!

Bacon Butties Locked Down by Rob Tuson

Once upon a time, a very strange time indeed, there lived three little pigs. These three unfortunate porkers were homeless. This was through no fault of their own, but because their pigsty had been requisitioned and was now being used as a temporary Covid 19 testing centre.

Faced with building his own new house, the youngest, laziest pig quickly gathered his stockpiled toilet rolls and made what he thought was a soft, strong, and very, very long house.

The middle pig clicked straight on to Amazon and got a flat pack MDF house delivered the very next day.

The eldest of the three pigs patiently queued for three hours at his local DIY store and eventually returned home with the supplies needed to construct a solid brick house.

Settled into his new abode the youngest pig was startled by a knock at his door. His online grocery delivery wasn't due until 6 weeks on Thursday, "So who could this be"?

The wolf outside cried, "Little pig, little pig, let me in."

"Not by the hair of my chinny chinny chin," was the reply.

"I'll huff and I'll puff, and I'll blow your house down," blasted the wolf. But try as he might it wouldn't budge. Flimsy as it was, the two-metre social distancing took the edge off the wolf's puff. Angrily he stormed off to try his luck elsewhere and the youngest pig hurriedly raced ahead of him to forewarn his older brother.

The scenario was repeated at the middle pig's house, but this time the wolf tried to be smart and brought a mask to avoid the need to socially distance. However, inevitably, the mask proved more of a hindrance than the two-metre distancing, so the pigs were saved and safe to dash off and warn their elder brother.

Risking a £100 fine, the wolf was now sufficiently hungry to disregard all government guidelines and regulations, but the brick house was never going to succumb to his huffing and puffing. Appearing disheartened, he left, and the pigs cheered, convinced of their safety.

However, thirty minutes later, they saw blue flashing lights outside.

Hesitatingly, they opened the door, whereupon a policeman and his lupine assistant PC issued them with a dispersal notice, as it just wasn't permitted to have three separate households together inside at one time. Thoughts of any bubble arrangements completely slipped their minds as they left the house.

Passers by later commented on the strange sight of a policemen and a wolf sat on a park bench observing social distancing whilst munching on freshly prepared bacon sandwiches.

Limerick by Jo Bennett

I went to the park with my Nan.
We travelled there in my old van.
She played on the slide,
and she laughed 'til she cried.
Said, 'I told you I could – and I can!'

Wellbeing by Janet Kilpatrick

(To the tune of 'My Favourite Things' from The Sound of Music)

Butterfly kisses
And first hints of springtime
Giggles with girlies and chilled glass of white wine
Sleep undiminished by irksome alarm
This is the secret to keeping my calm

Corrie on catch-up … without the commercials
Squares of dark chocolate
The hush of cathedrals
Crisp leaves a crunching 'neath wintry boot
That is the journey to peace absolute

Dogs breathing zephyrs through family car windows
Delirious dancing at jazz-funkster discos
Briny sea swimming
That's jellyfish free
These are the things that are pleasing to me

When the joy wanes
When the skies rain
When self-pity lands
I simply remember how special life is
And then everything's just grand

Ice Cream Van by Annette Pickering

It's not fair thought Michael, as he stood watching the other children queuing for ice-cream.

The van came every day, playing its tinkly tune of Popeye the Sailor Man. It was a hot sunny day and a cool ice-cream dripping with sticky raspberry sauce would really cheer him up.

The sound of the van's arrival had sent everyone scurrying home to ask for money. Michael had no-one to ask. His mum was at out at work. She'd had to get a job while Dad was working away. Well, that's what she said anyway.

He fiddled with the stuff in his pocket to take his mind off the ice-cream. A smooth pebble he'd found in the garden at Grandma's, a bit of string, a very grubby handkerchief, and an old penny. He kept the penny because the date on it was 1938. That was his dad's birthday, and he was going to show it to him when he came home.

It was a long time since he'd seen his dad and he could hardly remember what he looked like. He thought maybe he was like the man on the back of the penny. But his mum had said, "Don't be so daft, that's George the sixth and anyway he's dead."

Michael tried to think just when he'd last seen his dad. It was definitely before he started school. He'd had two teachers since then. The first one was Mrs. Roe. She was kind. But the second, Miss Batty was really strict.
He was glad it was the summer holidays, because when they were over, he'd have a new teacher.

Maybe Dad would be home by then and Mum wouldn't have to go to work, and he would have an ice cream.

Michael closed his eyes tight and squeezed the coin in his pocket while he made a wish

Me by Caroline Bradley

I am me.
I have always been me,
Since the start I have played this part, the role of me.
I have always known that I was born to play this part,
That no-one else could really do or be Me.
It is a big responsibility
To do it right, to do it justice & not mess it up.
To not fluff the unwritten lines or miss the unmarked cues,
To not be the one who everyone dodges & avoids on & off-stage,
Distrusts, mistrusts, can't rely on,
Can't believe what you've said & done.
To give me my dues,
I think I've done okay so far, overall if you don't count the mistakes,
The missed chances, the misused opportunities,
The misread, misunderstood, mishaps & the "What was I thinking moments".
I've ticked a lot of things off the bottomless bucket list,
And added more and I think
I've got the gist of what it's all about...kind of...pretty much,
With a bit of help from so & so and such & such.
I've taken notes & listened well,
I've looked to others not only myself,
I've followed direction & worked as a team with the cast of my life & theirs.
I've grown inside & outside and found my feet,
I've given of myself to others & learned how to treat them & me well.
I've taken the knocks & the punches, the high & the lows
The quick breakfasts & the long lunches,
The touring & travelling, the turning & the twisting of life & fate & love.

I've done a pretty good job overall so far, I think
All things considered,
Even if I say so myself in my internal monologue and silent soliloquy.
Always room for improvement though,
And I still think I have some way to go
Before I perfect my characterisation & fully find my
Deepest motivation and eternal raison d'etre,
The everlasting whys & wherefores &
The answers to the unwritten questions that we all know.
I am rehearsing still & so will be
Until my final curtain call.

Christmas Lament by Carol Rotherham

Christmas morning, early and bright,
Children awake from first light,
Peeped into their stockings and they found
that Santa had already been around.
"Look, a computer," the young lad said.
His words filled Mum with fear and dread.
Whirring and clicking, joystick in hand
the kids were transported to a new imaginary land.
"But stop, wait a minute," Dad wanted to know
when it was his turn to have a go.
Shift and format and memory and byte
the list of new words could go on all night.
There was a time when programme would mean
that Coronation Street would come on the screen.
Never again would Christmas be the same
with Dad, the kids and a new computer game.
Mother sobbed into her turkey lunch.
Thoroughly fed up with the whole bloomin' bunch.
Mother murdered them all in a spate of terror.
And later said "It was a computer error".

Limerick by Jenny

I know an old lady called Maisie
Who appears to be terribly lazy.
Spends all day in her flat
Sees no one and talks to her cat
I think she's quietly going stir crazy.

Granddad and the Piano by Linda Scholes

I sat on the old, rag rug in front of the hearth, looking into the fire. The flames licked around the coals, sending sparks up the chimney. I was holding Ruby, a long-legged doll in a bright yellow dress and hat. My mum had made this from the remnants of our kitchen curtains.

Granddad was in his usual armchair by the fire, pools coupon in hand, attention fixed on the football results being read out on the television, hoping it was his turn to win the jackpot. Grannie and Mum were seated at the kitchen table, tea brewing in the old brown pot, as they caught up on the gossip. Grannie was saying, "Honestly Betty, he never moves out of that chair unless I tell him. If it wasn't for me, the old man wouldn't go anywhere. I have to nag him to stir himself to get a wash and a shave these days."

Grannie always referred to Granddad as "the old man", who didn't look up once even though he was the subject of the conversation. Uncle Len was standing behind me, looking at his reflection in the mirror, adjusting his tie and smoothing down his hair with a liberal amount of hair oil. His friend, Albert, knocked at the door and Uncle Len, with a last glance in the mirror, said, "Bye all," and went out.

I sighed and thought, I might as well be invisible. Every Saturday we visited my grandparents and although I was happy to see them, there wasn't much to do once it got dark and I couldn't play outside. For a small child the evening seemed dull and boring inside with the adults. I had an idea of what I would like to do but I needed permission. I got up and stood near Grannie, waiting for her to notice me. "What is it, love?" she said.

"Please, could I go in the front room and play the piano?"

"Of course you can, I'll come and lift up the lid, it's heavy and if it drops, it could trap your fingers". Together we walked down the dark passageway to the front parlour. Grannie opened the door. Its hinges creaked. She switched on the light and drew the curtains. After opening piano lid, she left me alone and closed the door. I climbed onto the stool and put Ruby next to me. Randomly pressing the keys, I hoped to make a tune I recognised, but without any success.

I got off the stool and wandered around the room, examining the ornaments on the mantelpiece. There was a jug with a seaside scene showing Blackpool Tower and the slogan "Good Luck from Blackpool." Next to it was a shiny gold shoe which made me think of Cinderella. On either side was a pair of tall, glass vases, one of them had several dead insects in the bottom. Hanging from the picture rails and the backs of the chairs were my uncle's freshly ironed shirts. I counted ten altogether. He worked at the Post Office and had a clean shirt every day.

I was just about to return to the back room when the door opened, and I was surprised to see my granddad standing there. "How are you getting on with the piano playing?" he said. Granddad smiled at me, but he didn't say much as a rule, and I felt a bit shy about answering him. "I try to play something, but I don't know how to really."

Granddad said he could teach me if I wanted. I didn't even know he could play. Using the black notes, he played a simple tune. I was able to copy him, and I repeated it several times on my own. I felt really pleased. Granddad then played a tune I hadn't heard before. I sat quietly and listened. "What was it called, Granddad?"

"That's 'Lily of Laguna,' I used to sing it to your grannie when we were young." I couldn't imagine my grandparents ever having been young. It had turned cold in the parlour and Granddad shivered. He asked me if I was ready to go and join the others. "The Billy Cotton Band Show is starting on the tele," he said. I nodded, except I didn't enjoy the 'Billy Cotton Band Show' at all, but I thought it was polite not to say this and at least it was warmer in the back room. I took Granddad's hand, he switched off the light and, in companionable silence, we made our way down the dark hallway.

Mirror, Mirror on the Wall by Annette Pickering

Hello mirror, you're gleaming today.
Yes, I know you don't like that fellow Mr Sheen.
What's that? ....He spits at you.....
Well you certainly look better for his visit.
Anyway, you get your own back when he's been.
You always point out my shortfalls.
That spot on my face looks bigger and those so called laughter lines
look like gaping ravines.
I need what? Some sunshine.
It's funny you should say that mirror. I was thinking about going on
holiday.
Where to?..... Well Greece actually.
My friend Shirley went last month and didn't come back, she liked it
that much.
Oh, you know. I suppose it was wall that told you.
No. Who then?
Mediterranean Rock, who's he?
He sent you a postcard! I didn't see it.
Oh, that one, I remember it now, the beach looked heavenly. Even
though it was strewn with rocks.
What, you never go anywhere. Well I know, but you're so fragile,
you'd be shattered by the journey.
Anyway it's your job to keep an eye on him of the greasy spoon
brigade.
No mirror, I'm not taking him with me. I **need** a break and the only
place he wants to go is the pub.
I feel so trapped Mirror. There's got to be more to life than all this.
Washing sweaty socks, cooking, and cleaning up after him and all that
before I go to work.
Yes Mirror, I know you see it all, I know.

Perhaps next time he looks at you, you could point out that tide mark around his neck, the overhang on his belt and that stuff he calls designer stubble that hangs on his face.

Oh Mirror, there goes the door. This will cheer you up. It's our Sue. I know you like to look at a pretty young face.

Yes Mirror. I will ask her to be careful with the hairspray.

Yes Mirror, I know it gives you spots.

But don't worry; I'll get Mr. Sheen to call.

Greece or Grease by Annette Pickering

Hello Wall, it's me again.
Yes, I've decided to go.
I'm not going to stay one more moment,
I've got my flight booked, don't you know.

I picked up the tickets this morning.
I've borrowed a suitcase from mum.
I've pinched a bikini from Sue, it's the black.
And I'm going to have fun in the sun.

No Wall, I'm not going to tell him.
He'd only say "no, think again".
But I've left him a note in the chip pan.
When he reads it I'll be long gone by then.

The Peak (achieving success) by Jo Bennett

When he at last reached the summit
It took away his breath.
He felt he could open his arms
And he would be able to fly.
He drank it in with pleasure
And let time drift for a while.
Then slowly he began to see
Just how far he'd really climbed.
He saw the care he should take
Upon that high peak of his.
He pondered this for a while,
...............and then he smiled.

Toxic Waste by Annette Pickering

Cash was tight in the eighties. Kate was fed up with cooking the same old things every day. Trying to feed a family of six on a small budget was difficult.

When the new supermarket started giving recipe card ideas, Kate spotted one which she really fancied giving a try. The ingredients would be quite expensive. But she thought if she bought them bit by bit, leaving the fresh stuff to last, she would be able to cook it for their wedding anniversary.

No beans on toast or spaghetti hoops today. Kate carefully pan fried the onions and bacon, while the pasta gently boiled in another pan. She separated the egg yolks from the whites. She would use the whites later to make a lemon meringue pie, a family favourite.

When the fresh pasta, onion and bacon were cooked, she added the egg yolks, double cream, and grated parmesan. After seasoning the masterpiece was ready. She called the family to the table.

All were excited. Mum was cooking something new, and it wasn't out of a tin!

Kate had her fingers crossed they would like the creamy carbonara. She served it up on the best plates and sprinkled the fresh chopped chives on top. Well, it looked and smelled good. "Come on everyone, tuck in."

Kate looked round the table in dismay. Each member of the family was just pushing the food around their plates. Eventually her youngest son spoke up, "Sorry mum, it tastes like toxic waste."

Kate was mortified. He was right. Never again would she use parmesan cheese.

Seasonal Senses by Jean H

'Twas the week before Christmas. Six passengers waited under the canopy of the bus shelter for the bus that would take them to their destinations. As always at this time of the year the buses did come only later than usual when all the shoppers wanting to get rid of their packages and bags filled the vehicle to capacity.

Two men stood having a heated discussion whether it is possible to smell the snow that would arrive later that evening. "Rubbish, I don't believe a word of it, you're making it up!"

"I am not, it's perfectly true it has a certain flatness to its smell."

"Still rubbish."

The man who proposed the thought shrugged closer into his Parka and thought better not to answer as he wouldn't get anywhere trying to convince his friend.

Loaded down with bags and looking generally fed up with the pair and wishing for a hot drink one of the women who were waiting for the bus thought she might knock their heads together soon, so she decided to try and remember the time when her mother's mince pies came out of the oven, all brown and sparkling from the sugar sprinkled on each one. Mother made the best mince pies which were renowned in the family.

"Have one of Aunt Jessie's Mince Pies," she'd say to anyone visiting the house this time of the year, should they happen to call.

Lost in the world of yesteryear she was oblivious of the young girl standing next her who had a glazed look listening and nodding her head to whatever sound was coming through the headphones clamped on her head.

Propped on one of those ridiculous metal seats made for some-one's bottom that must belong to another alien planet as no-one on earth has a backside that shape, the elderly lady put her shopping trolley in front of her to stop her falling forward and sighed.

When will Christmas ever be celebrated as it was when I lived in that other world, white from September to March? I learnt many words that meant snow and the sound of the wind as snow flurries raced over the frozen ice was a comfort, as I knew when I heard it Father would not be long in coming home with a seal for our celebrations which was custom. I could imagine the seals soft skin making a cosy pair of Mukluks to keep my feet warm.

"I wish that bus would hurry up," she thought. "Why am I always so cold here in this damp strange part of this world where there are always grey skies? When I married my Mountie, I thought our life together would continue in the ways of my people, but governments decide what is best for others.

I have known the smell of snow for a lifetime and all the words for snow!"

Beauty is in the Eye of the Beholder by Jo Bennett

What's so great about being beautiful anyway? Everybody raves about beauty.

'Oh, you're so sleek and white',
'You're so smooth and elegant',
'I love the way you simply glide over the water!'

Just once in a while I'd like to quack, dunk and splash everyone and have some real fun. I love to watch the little ducklings – they're so cute and cuddly. No one wants to cuddle a swan! Even when they grow a little and start to look scruffy and spikey, they still have so much fun together. Who cares if your feathers stick out a bit and your neck's not long and elegant? You can splash and squawk and chase your friends all day long.

I try to tell the ducklings, 'Don't be in such a hurry to grow up – enjoy your young days – have lots of fun while you can.' They never believe what I say though. 'But you're such a beautiful swan – we want to be just like you'.

I have to preen and clean my feathers all the time. I glide around on the lake – or so they think – they don't see me paddling like mad below the surface! They only see what they want to – an image, not the real me. I used to quack and flap and chase my siblings. Mum used to come and rescue us if we got into trouble. Then at the end of the day, we would all get squashed up and cosy under her warm feathers. I dream of those times still.

There is one hope I suppose. One day I might have a family of fluffy, scruffy babies to look after and rescue from adventures. The thought of snuggling them all together in my very own nest would be something to look forward to.

'I'll need a mate of course. Maybe a bit of sleek beauty could come in useful after all!'

Choose Your Button by Annette Pickering

I think I'd have to choose the grey button.
I look at the flagstones that we set down years ago when we were
young and fit.
They stand now rocky and uneven on the patio.
If I just had to think about lifting and re-
laying them and it would be done.
Goodness me, I'd have the best garden in the world.
Even the leaves that fell in the autumn.
Beautiful colours of rust, red and gold. Are now a black slimy
hazardous mess.
Just waiting for some poor soul to slip and break a leg.
A simple thought would clean and clear them up.
Then maybe I'd press the yellow button, so I could read everyone's
thoughts as they watched the strange goings on in my garden.
"Is she a witch?" they'd think.
And I'd laugh to myself as I chose another button......

Nine Lives by Linda Scholes

You need a certain temperament for this kind of work. I consider myself very well qualified. I'm patient, calm, tolerant, optimistic and, when there is a crisis, I'm quick thinking – a problem solver. I abide by the motto on the agency, "Beside you, to guide you, on life's path."

My client, William Jones, has been keeping me busy. He is nine years old now. Yesterday he went missing. I just took a little break you know, caught up with the lads, when the call came through. His parents were frantic with worry because he hadn't come home from school. They were about to ring the police.

I knew where he would be. Sure enough, I found him down by the canal feeding the ducks with the leftovers from his lunch box. I told him his mum would be wondering where he had got to, and it was about time he went home. I accompanied him to his front door. The relief on Mrs. Jones face when she saw he was safe! I beat a hasty retreat, better than way, no questions asked.

Literally you take your eye of the ball for a minute and look what happens. While talking to you, William has kicked his football at Mr. Blakes' window and broken it, glass everywhere. The daft lad is reaching in through the jagged pane to try and retrieve it.

Hold on, William, your guardian angel is on his way.

A Dream Come True by Jenny

My name is Louisa Jane Matteson aged six and three quarters and I
live on our farm in the Yorkshire Dales with Mum, Dad, Grandpa and
my two elder brothers Luke and Nathan. It's Saturday. Brill, no school,
yippee, and it's the best day of the year for us, the Great Yorkshire
Show Day, hurrah, hurrah!

I could hardly sleep last night thinking about my important job
which is helping Dad show his prize-winning pedigree Charolais cows
and dreaming, maybe we could even win a rosette.

This year Dad is entering Daisy May and Sunshine in the
heifer and calf section and I'm going to lead Sunshine. The boys
usually go into the ring with Dad but this year they're helping Grandpa
with his sheep. So, it's my turn! Fab! I've got Nathan's white coat, it's
a bit big for me but that doesn't matter, because I've got my lucky star
mascot to pin on.

Daisy May and Sunshine are so beautiful and calm, their
creamy white curly coats perfectly match, and they have such big
velvety eyes and long floaty eyelashes. She's a good mum and I just
love them both. I have butterflies in my tummy but at last it's time to
finish off their grooming and line up. The noise is deafening and the
smells, wow! Sunshine licks my hand and fingers with her rough baby
calf tongue.

I hear Dad saying the competition is going to be tough because
there's a lot of experienced breeders in this section. He tells me don't
be too disappointed just enjoy the day. Dad says hold the reins up high
like him and just follow close. Mum says good luck and blows kisses.

The sun is high as we parade slowly around the ring, some
teams have trouble but Dad and Daisy May step by and we just follow.

Finally, we are selected to line up and the judges peer closely
at each pairing. I feel a bit sick, but Dad gives me a smile and thumbs
up. Slowly and seriously the judges talk and nod, clutching the
rosettes. Are they coming towards us?

Yes!!
First prize too, hurrah, hurrah!
Camera's flash and lots of congratulations follow.
My dream has come true.
A day for me to remember forever.

Reclaiming time by Glenda Davies

I rage against this suffering
Deceiver's swore would fade
Rainfall and I still cry for him
Repel the tide from taking him
To the ground where he is laid

New Season passes the window
The old leaves are swept away
Your smile turns to scorn on my passion
Locks the door and bids me to stay

But
I will rest against this moment
This memory shall not fade
Sunshine and I beam down on him
Splash in the tides still awaiting him
See
There is no ground where he is laid

*Poem inspired by TIME DOES NOT BRING RELIEF by Edna St
Vincent Millay*

Limerick by Jo Bennett

A soldier called Paul on guard duty,
Thought his comrades were rude and quite snooty.
So, he called them all out,
Fought a serious bout.
And his black eye is really a beauty!

A Questionable Journey by Annette Pickering

When are we going on holiday Dad?
When are we going away?
I thought that you said when I got home from school,
I thought we were going today.

Can Tommy come with us on holiday Dad?
'Cos his mum has said that he can.
And if we're going to Aberystwyth, Dad.
We can bunk up in their caravan.

I'm glad that you got the car fixed, Dad.
I'm glad that we're going today.
What time do you think we'll be there Dad?
Are you sure that were going the right way?

I really need something to eat, Dad.
It's a really long time since my dinner.
I could just eat a burger and chips, Dad.
LOOK, I'm just getting thinner and thinner.

We'll have to stop soon for the toilet, Dad.
I really can't wait anymore.
Is that the sea in the distance Dad?
Oh no! I've just wee'd on the floor.

Oh Dad, the beach is fantastic.
And the waves are all fizzy and white.
I'm glad that we've come here on holiday, Dad.
But I'm really tired now. Night, night!

The Covid Cokey by Caroline Bradley

You put your young un's out,
Keep your oldies in,
In out in out
You shake your germs about,
You do the Covid Cokey
And you turn around,
Lockdown's what it's all about.

Oh do the Covid Cokey,
Follow the science
Then go brokey,
3 word phrases
That make you chokey,
That's what it's all about.

You put your lives on hold,
Lies are sold,
In out in out
There are deniers all about,
You try to follow rules
That change ALL the time,
It makes you want to shout.

Oh do the Covid Cokey,
Try not to be too wokey,
Before it all goes up in smokey,
That's what it's all about.
We've had Brexit too,
To add to the goo,
In out in out
No-one knows what to do.

We got a deal that everyone hates
You can't deny
It needs flushing down the loo.

Oh do the Covid Cokey,
Round our necks it's a heavy yokey,
It's hard to even be that jokey,
Please God let it end...soon...

Limerick by Jo Bennett

The cat came in through the door.
She meowed that she wanted some more.
    I said, 'drink your milk first
    or you might die of thirst.'
But she tipped it all over the floor.

L.O.V.E No 3 by Caroline Bradley

Tiny nose, tiny toes,
Wet, warm, pink and raw.
That first weight of him on me,
My bare skin, drenched in the sweat
Of birthing
Our sweet miracle.
So vivid & real but
Almost unbelievable.
How on earth
Does this, can this
New life come from within,
From this mighty womb,
This bag of baby-making,
Factory of manufactured magic,
How, how, how?!
Truly, madly, deeply
I don't know.
Mother Earth looks up &
Ponders her mind-boggling magnificence,
While my thoughts skip along the horizon of imagination
Leaving me confounded.
I wonder the wonder
And it is wondrous!

A Big Adventure by Jean H

It was time to leave. After all I was grown up, wasn't I? Making the biggest decision of my life it was time to go. The world was mine! What was out there? I must admit I was a bit scared at such a great big world. I did not want any travelling companions as I was quite happy in my own company and that way, I would have control over it. Peering out from the shelter where I had grown up there was a lot to take in, where did the lane lead? Route 66 maybe? Or The Silk Road? Whichever, it would be a great adventure.

Starting out with trepidation I ventured forth on the lane leading away from all I had ever known. I hadn't gone far when I had this feeling that I was being watched. Gave me the creeps it did. Shoulders back, head up, I kept the thought that it was better to go onward and to stop being a wimp. At the end of the lane came a huge dilemma for me, do I go left or right?

If I go right there might be horrors waiting for me, if I go left, I might not have the courage to prove how brave I am! On the other hand, there might be even greater danger to the left! But as luck would have it and unknown to me, I had arrived at a cross ways in the lane. Simple! I will go straight on. I had heard a song being whistled one time, "Keep right on to the end of the road," and that's what I aim to do.

A car passed at high-speed going so fast the driver could not possibly have seen me at the side of the lane. After that I kept listening for any vehicle which might come along. The lane swung to the right with a slight uphill gradient and although I could cope with the incline I did wonder if it would get any steeper? But soon it started to level out which was great as I have never walked this far before and then, great joy the ground became steeper but the other way this time downhill!

I started to pick up speed and worried that I might go too fast and not be able to keep up with my feet and be able to stop. I didn't have brakes that cars have but wished I did have some. Faster and faster until I came to a grinding stop. The lane had led me back to where I had started from.

Feeling disappointed and relieved at the same time that my adventure had brought me back home again!

I scampered into the shelter and jumped into bed with my siblings all snug and warm. Mama mouse smiled at me as I too snuffled down to sleep after my adventure. Night, night!

The Truth by Annette Pickering

Harry, a young lad of thirteen years old,
Was fed up of being by his parents told
What to do, from the moment he got out of bed,
Wash your face, brush your teeth, comb that mop on your head.

One cold winter's morning, young Hal made a stand,
He had to do something, 'twas all out offhand.
He'd never before had the courage of youth,
But today was the day, that they would know **the truth.**

He jumped out of bed, on no doubt the wrong side.
He gazed round the room, and it filled him with pride.
It was his personality that flowed from the shelf,
From now on they'd know, this was Harry himself.

"You've got to eat food," cried his mum in despair.
When Harry said, "No," to the toast she'd prepared.
"You'll never grow up big and strong like your dad."
"You mean fat, overweight and a bit of a cad.

You lie to me, Mother, you've done it for years,
Like the 'spuds' that would grow in the dirt in my ears.
And if I ate carrots, I'd see in the dark.
And when my name's Smith, I can play in the park.

You said that if the wind blew, then my face would stick,
With that fact in mind, I stayed in for a week.
And when I ate apple pips, you said to me,
That deep in my stomach there would grow a tree.

All these things that you said, nearly brought me to tears,
But with lie after lie, you encouraged my fears.
I was too old to cry, these words filled me with rage,
And then in the next breath you said, act my age.

Harry's mother was sorry for all of the lies.
She listened intently, with tears in her eyes.
Her son stood before her, the essence of youth,
From now on from her, he would just hear the truth.

Town Centre Accident by Jo Bennett

The police officer ran to the old lady lying on the pavement. When he approached, he could see she was distressed. She had a bruise on her face and a grazed hand. He didn't know if she had any further injuries, but you always had to be careful, especially with the elderly. He estimated her to be around eighty or so years of age. She was alert and obviously angry and he noticed a skateboard only a few feet away.

'Skateboards,' he thought. 'Lethal things, so dangerous for pedestrians! They should not be used on pavements.' He knelt down by her.

'Don't try to get up madam. I've rung for an ambulance; we need to check you over – make sure there are no broken bones. I can see you have a few scrapes and bruises, does it hurt anywhere else?'

'Oh, I've had the wind knocked out of me!' she said. 'I hurt all over – just give me a minute or two to get my breath back – damned skateboard!'

'Yes, it's very upsetting madam. Can I ask your name?'

'Violet – Violet Jennings.'

'OK Violet – look, the ambulance is here now. They will check you over and take you to the hospital, just to be on the safe side. I'm going to confiscate this skateboard.'

'No, you leave it alone – it's my grandson's!' she shouted.

'What!!! You mean to say your grandson knocked you over and just left you here?'

'No – he wouldn't do that – he's a good lad. I just borrowed it – he doesn't know. I thought I might be able to get to the shops a bit quicker. I've seen the way he speeds along on it. I was ok until I hit a bump. These damn pavements are a mess, someone should report them!'

Limerick by Glenda Davies

My greedy big sister called Nellie
Each dinner she gorges on jelly
Down she comes bounding
To terrible sounding
Of her wibbly, wobbly Belly

October Musings by Estelle Weiner

I was manning the Welcome Desk and shop for Prevent Breast Cancer at the Nightingale Centre at Wythenshawe Hospital. Packs of Christmas cards had now been added to the variety of merchandise offered for sale. It was a jolt to the system - was it really that time of year again?

As the daylight hours shorten and autumn takes over from summer, I found myself beginning to think ahead to what we will be doing as we march onwards to December. October brings Halloween, November gives us Bonfire Night. With September morphing into October, we are assailed by the frenzy of Christmas and New Year. The corona virus pandemic has accompanied us through at least one of these events and by the end of the year, we will likely double that.

Trick and treat, then "penny for the guy" and serious musings by one and all about the weather that we can expect in the coming winter months. Whether in print or on television we are given a "Review" of the year just gone - sport, fashion, and sometimes rather sadly, eulogies for those loved and lost.

It was a particular busy morning with a varied cross section of patients awaiting their turn in their particular clinic. I became conscious of the fact that there were men patients, as well as quite young women with newborn babies. Others were obviously daughters accompanying mothers, sons accompanying mothers, friends with friends. A wall of photos of well-known and sometime famous fellow sufferers was described to me once as the 'wall of hope'.

No matter who or what, each individual goes on a personal journey towards a wish for a better year ahead. It is impossible not to be aware of the atmosphere of hope over adversity. The staff greet everyone with a cheery approach and smile; the patients often tell me how wonderful everyone is. Some are inspired to run fund-raising events of their own or make a point of supporting the shop and the cafe which in turn benefits the charity (PBC for short - also formerly known as Genesis). They feel individually connected and responsible for ensuring the needed research can continue.

In their own way, the hundreds of volunteers that make up the local and national caring community mirrors the folk I come across week on week. Some had celebrated birthdays and anniversaries alone instead of with loved ones, many went through the exact opposite, experiencing only sadness. It has been an unprecedented time of anxiety, a big-dipper journey of hope over adversity that we travelled as we tried to absorb this new Covid embracing way of life. Like the patients I come across - we found ourselves all in it together. Many forged new skills and relationships as they embraced the notion of meetings on WhatsApp or Zoom and learned the name of a new friendly face that brought needed goodies to their doorsteps.

New year, new beginnings, new hopes, new experiences, new ways of doing things.

The dictionary meaning of resolution says, 'the quality of being determined or resolute'.

Hopefully we can take this on board and take the New Year in our stride.

Don't Turn Around by Jayne Fallows

It was Lydia's first day in her new job at the library. She'd been introduced to all her new workmates, had a cup of coffee – no sugar, lots of milk - been shown where the toilets were and now it was time to start some proper work.

Mrs Bailey, the Chief Librarian, unlocked the door to the basement with an enormous key. "Before we start filing the music scores, I'll show you our collection of books on the supernatural. Our library was chosen as the one to buy all the published books on the subject, ghosts, spirits and so forth. Other libraries had to buy books on other subjects such as dogs or cats, but we got the spooky stuff. It's fascinating, really it is."

A long dusty corridor, lined with bookshelves, paved their way deep into the basement. Huge, leather-bound books balanced on wooden shelves, defying gravity.

"Look," said Mrs Bailey, "every book about the occult and the supernatural – every book ever printed on those subjects." She pulled a large book from the shelf. "Here," she said, "some of the covers are a bit scary. I'm not sure I'd want one of these on my bookshelves at home, it would give me the creeps."

Lydia tried not to look too closely at the book. The last thing she needed on her first day was to be seen running scared out of the basement because she'd spooked herself. Yes, she had a very vivid imagination. Everyone said so. It wouldn't take much for her to scare herself silly down here.

Mrs Bailey put the book back and spent some time going through what Lydia had to do to tidy and reference the music scores. "I'll leave you to it now," she said. "Shouldn't be too much trouble for you but if you get stuck just pick up the phone and dial 245 – that's the phone extension on the main desk – and I'll come back. So, you get cracking and I'll see you later."

Lydia started to sort through the music scores, humming quietly to herself. She knew she was going to love this job at the library. Books were her passion. What better place to spend her working life?

She ignored the noise at first, passing it off as the drone of traffic in the distance. Then she heard it again. It was a sound she couldn't identify. Voices perhaps? She strained to hear it more clearly but couldn't define exactly where it was coming from. "Mrs Bailey is that you," she called. Nothing. No answer.

She walked down the corridor to try and identify the sound. But it just got louder. She imagined voices saying, "Don't look behind you. Don't turn around." The blood in her veins chilled. The supernatural book collection was right behind her. "Don't turn around," said the voices again. Her feet wouldn't move. She couldn't breathe. Sweat damped her hair, sticking her fringe to her forehead. The noise was getting louder. "Don't turn around. Don't turn around."

She should call for Mrs Bailey. She looked at the phone. It was at least twenty paces away. She measured the distance with her eyes, but it could have been twenty miles because there was no way she could move her feet to get to it. Blood and movement were gone from her legs. Her heart would surely burst through her chest it was beating so hard.

"Hello, anybody there?" said a man's voice, making her heart beat even faster. "Hello," said the voice. "I've come to fix the central heating. I bet the noise from that broken pump has been driving you crazy."

Limerick by Glenda Davies

My silly wee friend name of Brenda
Cried out "I have lost my suspender!"
Cavorting with Jack
She heard something snap
A garter was all I could lend her

A Feast of Memories by Maggie Waker

Vesta products came into our lives in the 60's. Mum, not an adventurous cook, decided to take us on a world tour with Vesta. We'd never been abroad. Scotland was as far as we'd ever been, so Vesta was exciting and very surprising.

Inside the packet was a strange mix of murky dried and powdered substance, wrinkly bright green peas, little brown grains of mince that were as hard as bullets, and tiny shrivelled prawns all mixed with an unidentifiable orange powder.

There was something about it that reminded me of the magic painting books that we had as little children. But this time it wasn't so much a change of colour on the page as a transformation of texture springing to life when water was added in the saucepan.

A small packet of rice was included with careful instruction – just as well (since the only rice we had eaten before was baked into a sweet rice pudding). Illustrated on the back was how to serve this exotic dish. An appetizing sauce surrounded by a ring of fluffy white rice.

In those days we always managed with a pack for two people even though there were actually three of us to enjoy this special delight.

Forty years later, at Mum's 80th birthday we gave her a packet of Vesta curry. Oh! How she laughed ...

Thomas' Dilemma by Annette Pickering

Thomas faced a dilemma. At eight years old, he didn't really know what a dilemma was.

He knew, because he'd learnt at school, that plastic was bad for the environment. It was causing major pollution in the sea, and it was killing fish.

There was a river running behind his house. He could see it from the bottom of his garden. This same river ran behind his grandad's house a couple of miles away. Last summer Thomas spent a lot of time at Grandads. They'd sat on the riverbank with fishing nets, catching all the rubbish as it floated by. He'd caught plastic carrier bags, fizzy pop cans, beer cans and all sorts of other bits and pieces. Grandad did this every day. He said there were some 'dirty beggars' about, all too lazy to take their rubbish home.

Of course, now, because of this corona virus thing, Thomas was stuck at home. His school was closed, and he wasn't allowed to visit Grandad in case he spread the virus. To make things worse, last night's freak storm had brought the telephone lines down. So, Thomas couldn't even ring him.

Grandad didn't have a mobile phone. He didn't have any truck with all this 'techno stuff'. He said, "The robots were trying to take over the world."

So here was Thomas's dilemma. He thought if he wrote a message to Grandad, telling him that mum was sorting the phone problem. He could put it in his empty lemonade bottle and throw it over the fence into the river. The bottle would float down, and Grandad would fish it out. He knew that Grandad would mutter about the 'dirty beggars', but at least he'd know his telephone was going to be fixed and Thomas's bottle wouldn't go on to cause more pollution.

It was four o'clock when the phone rang. It was Grandad. He was thanking Mum for getting the phone fixed. Mum looked puzzled. "How did you know I was sorting it?" Grandad laughed down the phone, "Thomas sent me a message in a bottle."

Property Tycoon by Rob Tuson

I'd never envisioned myself being a landlord. My parents were staunch renters, but Mike said, go on give it a go, you might even enjoy it. London was the place to be, so I picked my car up and set off into a grey and dreary November day. Through the recently gentrified East End I drove, where areas were up and coming, retaining little of their Jack the Ripper Whitechapel heritage. Our first stop was to pick up Aunt Geraldine from Kings Cross Station. Coming out of a side street on to the busy Euston Road that passes in front of the station, I took a real chance with the oncoming traffic and narrowly avoided running over a small dog who had strayed from her owner.

Aunt Geraldine was something big in the civil service, so before we could get going properly, we had to pop into her Whitehall offices to pick up some important papers. Outside the offices on the street, I spotted a £10 note on the floor. I looked round furtively, but there was no one watching, so I slipped the note into my pocket. It felt like it was my birthday. It was difficult to manoeuvre the car from where we had parked it, but remarkably for central London it was free parking, so I didn't want to complain. I wanted to push on to the business in hand, but Geraldine insisted we stop for lunch. We ate at an Italian restaurant close to the bustling Leicester Square and overlooking the Odeon cinema where all the big red-carpet premieres are held.

Then it was off to the property we were viewing.in one of the more affluent parts of London.

The traffic down the main Oxford Street shopping thoroughfare was horrendous and too busy chatting, I absentmindedly jumped a red light. My heart sank as I spotted the flash of the camera trap. Another fine and three points on my licence, but minor in the overall scheme of things. It was hardly an imprisonable offence. This part of London was what I'd really had in mind when Mike had first suggested getting involved in the property business.

Down the affluent and wide Park Lane we drove and swept into the iconic Mayfair. Parking spaces were at a premium, but we found one close to a very posh looking hotel and pulled up outside. A finely dressed man came over to our car and held the door open. We thanked him, but he then insisted that we owed him £2,000 and must pay up in cash immediately or the game was up.

We turned out our pockets but had nowhere near enough and at that point I realised that playing Monopoly was nowhere near as much fun as Mike had promised.

The Collector by Jo Bennett

Another picture? Glory be!
There is no room; there cannot be!
They fill the walls and line the stairs,
They stand on easels, lean on chairs,
Those men and women, towns, and trees,
Flowers, beaches, skies, and seas!
The pastels, soft in greys and blues,
The watercolour's gentle hues.
And brighter, oils, how they portray
The sun, the light, the changing day.
You have a need to hold them all,
To have them close, fill every wall.
Those images you hold so dear,
How can you keep them ever near?
How will your home contain this band?
How can you make the space expand?
I'll share my secret, give you ease.
The simple answer's bound to please.
Those you have loved, the things you've seen,
The places where your heart has been,
Those wondrous skies and changing seas......
The walls of your soul are endless....
And hung with these.

My day at the Coronation by Estelle Weiner

It was 1953, and I was eleven years old. My favourite Aunty worked in central London in an office on Regent Street.

It was Coronation Day; June 2nd and I was super excited. Aunty had a special ticket to get both of us onto the street and into the building. The tall wooden double doors at the entrance had a half moon glass window above them. The caretaker had erected a couple of stepladders with a plank of wood across the top between the two. This was our viewing platform, and it would enable us to see over the heads of the crowds outside on the pavement and watch as the magnificent procession passed by. Some people on the pavement had periscopes they looked into which also gave them a higher up view.

Despite the rain, everyone was in festive mood. It was really thrilling and although we'd had to get up very early to enable us to gain access to the offices, the hours just flew by.

Once the procession had passed us, we went upstairs to one of the offices. Someone had managed to rig up a television and we all gathered around it so that we were able to watch the fabulous crowning ceremony of Queen Elizabeth II in Westminster Abbey.

The memories of that day still make me smile - it was so very special.

Open Door by Caroline Bradley

Here I stand...in an open door,
My sleeveless soul cupped in my wavering hand,
Looking for escape.
My heart is close to breaking
Point as I carry
Heavily the scars of the sorrows that surround me.
I dream of soaring out,
Light and lifted,
Free of fear and climbing.
I can feel it so close, warming me to the bone,
The letting go, the moving on out, the up up and away of my favourite
dream.
I will no longer hold all the burdens so close
And let them slowly devour me inside out.
Nor let the worries that shroud me in darkness
Be such strong chains,
Fixing me to this spot in time and space,
Squeezing the wellness from my organs,
And stopping my internal sight
From revisioning me with clarity.
These times have been tough for all of us
But we can still choose to move into the
Light.
I am here...now...
Standing in a doorway,
Seeking the decider for my next move.
Will it be down and out or out and proud,
Loud and strong,
A lyrical birdsong on a wandering wing.
I am scared, I know I am,
Afraid of what I don't know,

Can't control, can't predict,
But I need to take the risk.
A simple doorway can offer
An infinity of possibilities
And I only need one
To take me on.
Just one small step forward...
And I am through.
I reach my arm backwards...
And pull you through with me.

The Sun Crossword by Jean H

My friends Jane and Noel had a thing about entering competitions which they did with gusto regularly. You name it they entered for it no matter how bizarre, even if they did not really want the product being the winning prize.

"Somebody has to win," was their favourite reply when asked, "Why, do you do so many competitions"? Chocolates, Dog Foods. It really didn't matter what the product was. Every week whatever was in magazines or newspaper or even on goods bought at the supermarket they would save up the competitions and sit down on a Sunday and fill in the coupons etc. Thinking of witty words to fulfil the criteria of creating wording that would portray the said companies' product to its full glory passed many a wet Sunday in front of the fire.

Would their endeavours be recognised as the one true passage that would win them the prize on offer or was this a waste of time? Some-one has to win!

Being home-brew enthusiasts, they spotted a competition for Courvoisier Brandy. How could they resist this one? With pen and paper close at hand the way was clear! Take the best shot and go all out for it!

There was many scratching of heads, lots of paper discarded on the floor and the Sunday roast was forgotten about. The rule for them was to post their efforts as soon as possible so they could not start correcting the entry in any way. It was coming back from the post box that the Sunday roast was remembered. Good job they had plenty of baked beans in the cupboard.

Weeks went by and they had almost forgotten their entry. Yet another failure to win. When through the letterbox came a long envelope with the result of the competition they had so painstakingly written and re-written. That vital entry to Courvoisier Brandy. THEY HAD WON!

After the initial shock of winning the Prize from Courvoisier panic set in! Can we get time off work for those dates? Who will look after the children? With these problems sorted they then looked at the instructions.

A chauffeured limousine would take them to Manchester Airport and fly them to France by private jet. On landing a car would take them to Courvoisier Chateau to have the pleasure of seeing the making of the brandy. The trip lasted a few days which were absolutely fabulous being wined and dined like royalty. Came the time to return to the U.K. The return journey would be all taken care of.

When they had a time to reflect. Did all that brainstorming really win us this adventure?

Asking how they had won, "Was it our witty description of the finest brandy in the world?"

"Oh no, your name was just pulled out of a hat!"

They never won anything else again but what a prize to win, eh?

Limerick by Jo Bennett

There was a young sailor called Frank,
Whose captain said, 'You walk the plank.'
So, he laughed and jumped in,
'cause he knew he could swim.
But he drowned when he actually sank.

The Weekly Shopping Trip by Jenny

As she walked through the sliding doors at the front of the shop, she jumped as a man reached out and touched her on the arm. "Excuse me madam, can I have a quiet word?" Hilda felt her cheeks burning, as he showed her his card; STORE DETECTIVE it said.

"I have reason to believe you have taken goods from the store without paying for them. Please come back into the store to the Manager's office."

Hilda knew she had checked everything through the self-service machine and had the receipt to prove it. "Here young man, carry my groceries my arm is aching and mind, I expect a complete apology and compensation once you check my bag."

The bag of meagre groceries was turned out in front of the manager and the local bobby and the three of them checked the goods off. Potatoes, bottle of milk, past sell by date bread, biscuits, tomatoes, a couple of tins and some bacon. All checked against the receipt. "Well, satisfied?" She demanded. "Now I want my apology and over that loudspeaker thing."

"Turn out your pockets, please." Indignantly Hilda slammed down some crumpled tissues, a few coins, keys, her bus pass, and a couple of boiled sweets. Nothing for them there.

"Please unzip your coat, madam." Slowly the zip was undone, coat off and Hilda stood before them in her loose shirt and trousers.

"Raise your arms please, madam."

"This is ridiculous," she cried. But as she moved something fell to the floor; there lay a squashed packet of fish fingers. "Oops!" Hilda said nonchalantly, "Wherever did those come from?"

"From under your shirt, Hilda, and I'm going to have to charge you with shop lifting from this store again but first we will ring your daughter to get her to come and collect you."

"Aw well," she sighed, "and I was looking forward to a nice fish tea tonight."

Singing by Anne Thompson

When Bill was first diagnosed with Fronto Temporal Dementia (FTD) he loved to sing. His favourite vocalist was Elvis Presley, which was odd because before diagnosis Elvis wasn't on his "most played list." At the day centres he attended he would often perform at the mike with the professional entertainers "Can't help falling in love with you," was usually his song of choice. Whenever I went to pick him up the staff would tell me how good his singing had been and how much he enjoyed performing a solo.

Now one of the worst symptoms of FTD is a total lack of empathy for others and so Bill never reacted when one of our special songs was played as he had done before his diagnosis. Then Christmas 2019 his Day Centre put on a concert and gave Bill the star solo, singing "I can't help falling in love with you." I was stood at the back of the room and as he sang the title words, he pointed towards me.

A truly heart wrenching moment!

Printed in Great Britain
by Amazon

71219537R00073